Don't Mention

Pirates

SARAH McCONNELL

BARRON'S

Scarlet Silver
had a secret that
nobody could guess:

not her mom,

not her dad,

not her brother Cedric,

not even Grandpa Jack...

Now the Silvers were
a very ordinary family —
except that they lived in
a ship-shaped house.

Yes, really **ship-shaped.**

Scarlet's mom inherited it from
her famous pirate Grandma...

...Long Joan Silver.

There was one rule in the Silver house – and only one rule:

Don't mention Pirates, on account of the terrible luck that befell Grandma Silver when she was accidentally eaten by a giant shrimp!

oops!

From that day onward,
No Pirates was the rule.

But that wasn't easy for Scarlet...

...because secretly she wanted to be a **pirate!**

Scarlet loved the smell of sea air.

And was excellent at making people walk the plank.

She'd even taught
Bluebeard, her
parrot, to squawk,

"Pieces of Eight."

But Mom and Dad were not proud. "Don't mention pirates," they said very loud.

The thing that all pirates, including
Scarlet, loved best was

searching for treasure.

So Mr. Silver built Scarlet a treasure detector.

She found **odds** and **ends**
and
bits
and
pieces,
but nothing
exciting.

Until one Tuesday,
beep, beep, beep, the detector went off!

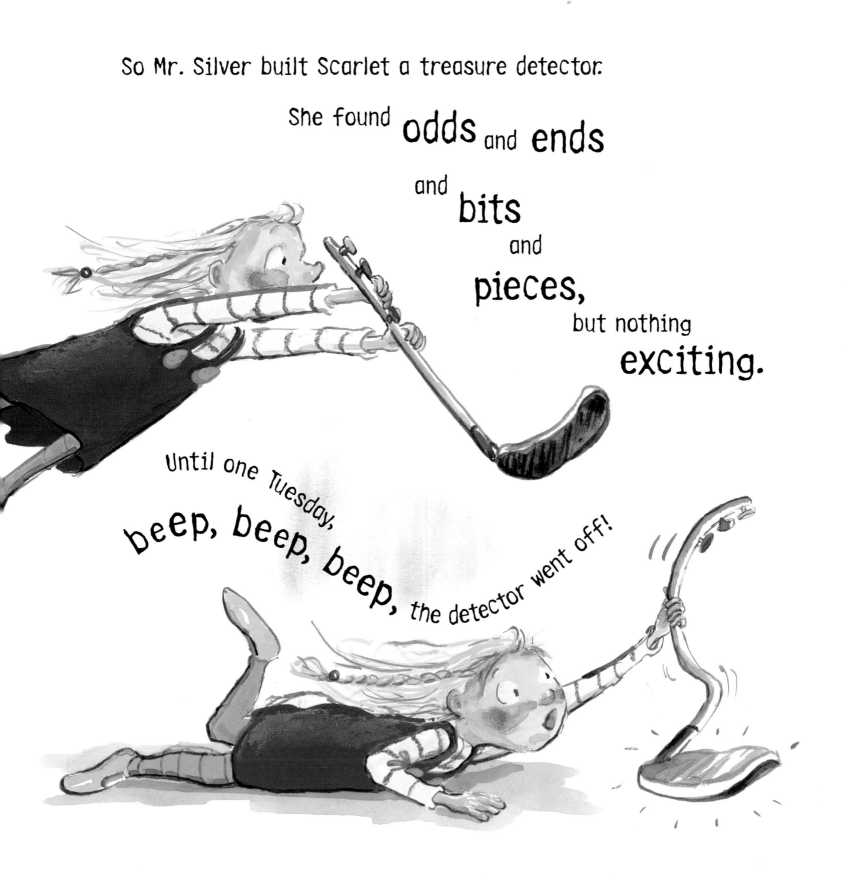

"Bless my barnacles," said Scarlet. "I've found gold!"

And she ran into the house
to tell the others.

"It can't be real gold," said Dad Silver.
"Yes, it can," said Mom.
"Eureka!" shouted Cedric.
"Call Grandpa," said Scarlet so excited she
forgot he'd gone fishing with one-eyed Scott.

They all jumped up and started to search
for something, anything to dig up the gold.

At six o'clock,
they took a break:
ship-shaped
cookies on a
ship-shaped plate.

Ahaa, just what
pirates eat,
thought Scarlet.

They began to dig and
the sun beat down so
they tied handkerchiefs
around their heads.

Hmmm, just what **pirates**
wear, thought Scarlet.

They kept on digging,
till the sun went down.
"Bedtime," said Scarlet yawning.
"Not till we find the loot!" said Cedric.

Ha ha, just how **pirates**
speak, thought Scarlet
and left them to
their digging.

The next morning, Scarlet got a shock!
"Why are you wearing eye patches?"
she demanded.
"We were throwing mud pies," replied Mom.
"Aye, and these make perfect eye
protectors," added Dad.

But Scarlet wasn't fooled.
"You look just like—"

"Don't
mention
pirates,"

the others roared.

The Silvers dug and dug, until they could dig no more.

"There must be more gold," said Dad.
"Aye!" agreed Mom.
"It'll be there," said Cedric,
pointing to just below the house.
"Wait," said Scarlet, but they
didn't listen. Dad grabbed his shovel.

"Knock it off, ye landlubbers!"
shouted Scarlet,
"or the house will fall down."
"Sufferin' seagulls," said Mom, Dad, and Cedric.
"She's right."

They staggered inside
and flopped on the couch.
"Well, we've still got the
nugget," said Scarlet.

Just then the back door flew open.

"Ahoy!" said Grandpa Jack.
"I'm back, what's that
you've got there?"

"My heroes," he said. "You've found me gold tooth."
And he popped it, click, back into his mouth.

Before anyone could say a word, Grandpa said,
"What's happened this week, you look just like a bunch of p—"

Suddenly, there was a

CREAK, then a
CRACK,
then a...

...SPLOOSH!

"Pirates, that's what we are,"
said the Silvers. And as soon as
they said it, they knew it was true.

"Hoist the main sails!"
shouted Scarlet.

And off they sailed in
search of treasure, because
that's what pirates do!